Marigold

Manasvini Duggal

AF517521

BlueRose ONE.com
Stories Matter
NewDelhi • London

BLUEROSE PUBLISHERS
India | U.K.

Copyright © Manasvini Duggal 2026

All rights reserved by author. No part of this publication may be reproduced, stored in a retrieval system or transmitted in any form or by any means, electronic, mechanical, photocopying, recording or otherwise, without the prior permission of the author. Although every precaution has been taken to verify the accuracy of the information contained herein, the publisher assumes no responsibility for any errors or omissions. No liability is assumed for damages that may result from the use of information contained within.

BlueRose Publishers takes no responsibility for any damages, losses, or liabilities that may arise from the use or misuse of the information, products, or services provided in this publication.

BlueRose ONE.com
Stories Matter
NewDelhi • London

For permissions requests or inquiries regarding this publication,
please contact:

BLUEROSE PUBLISHERS
www.BlueRoseONE.com
info@bluerosepublishers.com
+91 8882 898 898
+4407342408967

ISBN: 978-93-7542-894-7

Cover Design: Alex Paiva
Typesetting: Sagar

First Edition: April 2026

To my Family, precious both

of blood and of choice.

And

To my Dad,

I hope this finds Him

wherever He has chosen to rest.

Preview

The conception of this book began two years ago, at the very beginning of 2024. Initially meant to be presented as a raw collection of grief, I decided that it must be published after the completion of my final undergraduate semester abroad. But as the idea gestated, and the months went on, it became clear that the experience of grief I wanted to present did not exist within a single emotion, or even within a certain period of time. It was constant and ebbing; even today, it comes and goes.

It is like the waves of a *vast*, silent ocean.

So, I decided that there would be virtue in waiting for this book to manifest itself further.

Time went on, seasons came and went, and the grief still stayed. But, so did other experiences. Changing seasons, Love in many forms, Life in its youth and surprises, new cities that were once home away from home, and the relief of being back where I truly belong- all ebbing and flowing into what I can now see as the newest chapter of my life. And so, was born Marigold.

Named after a flower of spirituality, of sacred times and piety. A bright orange flame that presents itself as a heart ablaze. Warmth in the Winter. Sunshine in its petals. My father's favourite flower, the one that surrounded me after his death. The duality of it within the Hindu tradition, of decorating homes with its garlands during times of celebration, and times of loss.

Marigold, its garland around the many seasons of my life.

Contents

Prologue

Hushes lined the spaces within which we stood, within the confines of the hospital room which an hour ago was ablaze with machinery and a wailing child, within the hospice of the open wound that was inflicting itself on us and everyone rushing here from their homes, within the seat of the car where we, where I, already knew to accept what was to come.

I found you, on your knees and hushed, and I knew my life was about to change.

Months later, I drew a picture of an eclectic pyre, and my vague figurine standing by its side. I drew the dotted stars of Ursa Major, the Saptarishi, rising from the watery inferno on my page and on the page above, they transformed into marigolds.

Marigolds are meant to light up the path for the dead, to find their way back to those they loved. For those of us who live, marigolds light up the distance we have walked away from that same moment, for us to retrace the same path.

I imagine a bridge of marigolds rising up from the embers of that pyre into the skies, my only solace when I try to reach out to you in the night. Wherever you are, I hope the brightness of fiery, orange flowers can always lead you back to me.

Winter

of Cremations, of a Deep Blue Dark;

the Constant Search for Light

Delay

I delay writing about your death in any manner of prose. Not for the threat of abandonment, I know you did not mean to. But I never wanted this to be inspiring. I never wanted to try and live despite it all.

I never wanted you to fuel my art, the one thing that I strive to keep so alive.

Flame

Fire has always mesmerised me. We live so afraid of its touch, and yet to watch it is to watch all the orange of the cosmos in a single column of flame. Every year during the *Pujas* we would hold, the early morning burn in my eyes would be taken in, entirely, by the flames licking the small pyre of wood in our home. I would see you pour the *ghee* over your parents' immortal souls, as I would find intrigue in the glow of those flames.

I thought I had time before we would burn those flames for you. The fire I lit in front of a hundred consumed me as much as it did you. I am glad you were not there to see me accept that threshold.

"*I just love watching flames*". You said that in a moment of calm, just 12 days before, in the light of warmth, drink, and peace, before we ushered in the new year together. Warmth and nothingness come through flame. Happiness and desolation, by orange and tips of blue. I heard your words ringing all through, as I lit the pyre that would consume your mortal flesh, leaving nothing the next morning but ash and charred body; bits of bone. Fire warmed and ruined me that month. I have nothing of you to physically keep.

I thought I had time before I had to be the one to pour the *ghee.*

Fire trickled out your inner child. Fire burned away some of mine. The child that belonged to you for twenty-one years. Every time I will look through flames, I will picture you. Burning away, silent, cold and whole. And me, pouring life into the flames that would take you away from me.

*E*very living part of me
still holds onto you.

January Smoke

A lexicon of seasons, and away we go,

to and from that starching

January snow.

To and from

the method in the madness,

the trail of white flowers in the morning cold;

they trail my way to the rest of my fold.

I smell of jasmine, as my home smells of lilies and wooden smoke,

I waver at the sunlight falling in through my broken windows, onto my tainted floor;

I waver at the flowers,

guising the darkness that falls along with their shadows.

All day, every day,

a triad of white flowers, and the smell of scented, January smoke.

Morning Glory

This, is where love trickles down.

Like raindrops on an open window,

like monsoon down on frosted storms.

Like

gold;

Orange, for the love of colour,

purple for the love of warmth,

and pink in most of these corners, because why stop

if not in the name of manicured mysticism?

My mother bunches the flowers

in colours where they seem most at home;

oranges with pinks,

purples with cream in a vase of blue,

translucent, oceanic blue,

and whites in the corner

for the love that comes with loss.

white, for the love of all that comes with loss.

And me?

I love the pieces of personality

that bloom and change with every vase.

Morning lily, *morning glory*;

What is the story that comes

when my mother changes the colour of this love

with next week's trickling,

frosted, watery, winter sun.

The Very First Sign of Winter

It is the first day of the year, the last week of an ending October, when one can first feel the incoming darkness of the winter dusk; the slight, slight glow of pink from the setting sun, mingling with the soft orange of my vanilla candlelight. And all around, for the first time this year, the rising feeling that comes with the sudden deep blue darkness, of an evening that has come much too soon. Nothing screams "*winter*", nothing whispers "*loneliness*" deeper, than this deepening blue, sweeping around that orange candlelight.

A loneliness that is not "bad", a warmth in the light that is not "good", but the first signs of an ancient, primordial, Western cold. A force deeper and darker than most, the kind that a small candlelight struggles to keep at bay, but always this feeling of inevitability that it will *try*. Regardless of the Big Deep Ocean of cold, cold dark outside that window, and in my room.

Try, as we too do, with our fuzzy sweaters and warm cinnamon cookies that keep us happy at night. But October is a month of dusk. It is ethereal, in the darkest way. A reminder to celebrate the morbidity of Halloween and to understand that the darkness outside will not always stay where it belongs, and that all we can do is watch, and light our candles anyway.

Watch the shadows colour the deep, midnight blue with flickers of orange and Warmth.

Candle Light

This year's sun, it better last.

This year's rain, I hope,

is soft.

It has been a year, and some more,

since I began my search

for gold, for sanctuary in a song;

the kind that sings

of silver in the clouds.

This year's moon, I wish to be full,

and I hope that it becomes easier to float with the tide.

I keep forgetting to remember

how hard it is to keep up with the tide

This year, I will continue my search

for serendipity somewhere inside;

the four-fold

of incense laden with white marble tiles,

and my first time reading the sign

on a wooden church signboard,

"Light a candle for whoever you miss"

Light a candle, for maybe they miss you too

I did,

and I keep forgetting to remember

how this year, the cold was harsh,

but the rain was still soft as snow.

Orange Sky

This grey November sky

tries to be so cold, yet it stays true

to the deep orange inside.

When you look at it close,

why is it that no one pretends to know

what the sunlight looks like anymore?

Why does the summer turn blue

before we get to watch it turn to gold?

I think my salvation lies

in this morbid dream, lined with the gold that I filled inside;

gold so fragile and brittle,

until I looked up, and I saw it right there.

Dead centre, in the light.

Lined underneath the grey, I did not know I stood beneath an orange sky.

Till I looked beyond November's cold.

Gold Peaked Sun

Always

I blaze like a chemtrail over my world.

The seven seas, over

the blue horizons of snow peaks,

the glowing pink novelty of the sun,

thinking to myself,

"This, right here, hurts".

Yet

"This journey really could be worse";

how lucky I am to feel lonely, with a view.

But now

that I see you

in the setting eyes of this gold peaked sun,

I realise,

I would choose you over all the beauty of this earth-but, a "thank you" to the world,

for trying anyway.

Sunblind

For the cold, cold scent of summer's hail,

for the end coming up the tip of winter's tail,

I am, for once, craving the last days of warmth,

for the start of something anew.

And in the last heaving breaths of summer's climaxing gaze,

in the tiptoe-ing touches of winter's cold, saving grace;

in this Miracle of Movement, I feel sunblind.

sunsets held in the lasting graze of your touch.

Sparkle

I was walking back home the other day, late evening under a blue, navy haze; the navy of a premature dusk that slowly blends in with the colours of midnight. *I wonder why we call it "midnight blue", when midnights in November to February are nothing less than the inkiest, milkiest black.* Against this navy, blue and black of a shivering, bruised sky, the one saving grace that comes with the impending winter bloom is the glorious twinkling of these thousand stars on earth. Strung up all over the city and its crooked alleyways, the lights above reflect the ever-present metaphor that even in the growing dark, there is always the shimmer of a path guiding us home.

Sometimes I think about the nature of my most obscure sorrows, and one of them I feel reflects this deep-blue winter dusk sky. I think of "forever", and sometimes I think of the things that we loved and those that, in their love, hurt us. Hurt us, inspired us, and showed us where to go next- where, within our palms, to place our passions in, and ultimately, *I think about how these are the very things we seem to forget.* I look at these lights urging me to walk outside despite the cold, find my way to and from home, and I think of all the things I have loved and lost that would have urged me to do the same. *Things I do not remember anymore*, the taste of which lingers like the flakiness of a vivid dream that passes by the second we wake up. Things that once meant the world and more, but now only exist in the sparkle of the experiences they left behind. It is easier to remember "how" I got here, but not as easy to remember "why", and sometimes, I grieve what I do not know. I miss what I do not remember, and I still chase that sparkle the way

I chase a dream in the mornings. But the silhouette of my once tangible love and hurt fades away just as fast as it came.

In the simplest of ways, I try to follow the obscurity of my grief, and I know I miss things, and people, and feelings that were important and bigger than the world once. But all I get back are shadows. And a sparkle.

I miss what I do not remember; I think we all do. And I feel like stardust when I think of how strange it is to be at a point where I feel a nostalgia that I cannot trace. Like a memory of a dream I do not remember. Nothing feels quite as heavy as the feeling of a lost memory that I cannot recall. And so, there is grief. An ever-knowing, ever-consuming loss. And yet, the warmth of something I forged with it.

The sparkling legacy of a thousand memories, lost in time.

Time

I had a dream again,

just like many I have had before, where, like a memory overplayed, I *remembered* you. As with all these dreams I have had before, with a ticking sense of accepted doom, I held my elation.

"It is just a dream". Within my lucidity, I spoke.

I know this like a moment rehearsed, because it is far too real to remember you are not there anymore- A truth I knew to my core when I saw you lying on that floor.

I am grateful, because my dreams have never allowed me to pretend otherwise.

Last week though, weeks since I last saw you,
in a room full of people, I interrupted your speech- it was about me.
"*My daughter can do anything she puts her mind to*". "I try", I said,
"but, you really should know, you're not here to see it anymore".

You hugged me and said, "*I know*".

And in that lucidity, I held onto that hug and stretched it beyond the dream wanted me to. That hug felt right, and I tried, for once, to really let myself breathe it in. I held on.

Until it was time to let go again.

Firefly

There it is, the *slight*, slight gauze of your gaze,

the tiniest specks of grace

that come floating by like embers in the night.

The flecks of sparkles

that trail behind fireworks in the sky,

fairy dust in pixie hollow,

the sweetness of starlight I am made to swallow-

It is everything I can do,

to keep myself from thinking of you

in only one *shade of gold.*

So, I think of this as lanterns

in the blue-black of an inky night.

The floating spectacle

of an army of dragonflies,

or the glow of jellyfish, rainbowed

under the silver of the moon.

I swallowed the whole of the moon

and washed it down with the entirety of you.

The music, the kindness, *the light*

of a single, solitary, golden wire.

The buzz

of a friendly little firefly,

against my crackling, lonely

campfire.

Sometimes

In this graveyard of sad streams,
I walked through the pinks of a baby's dream,
and I knew it was time to go.

Just kids a minute ago,
broken hearts and broken souls,
sometimes running away is a moment of truth,
not a moment being left alone.

And sometimes, nothing feels better
than the promise of spring after a winter of aching sores.
Sometimes, it feels so lonely to even know
when it's time to let spring in,
and leave the winter to its ashes and bones.

I am right where you left me,
I am still trying to walk through this threshold,
and I have only your fingers to let go.
It is time to let spring in,
and leave the winter to your ashen bones.

White Flowers, White Stars

i. I love the sudden, glorious feeling of the sun in my eyes, the fleeting, cooling freshness of a breeze against my skin. I love the sounds of the road and sky wherever I go, and this winter, like winter last, I come back home, and I carry with me the sunshine and wind of a colder, newer shore. I guess some things never change.

ii. I love the scent of fresh flowers, I love their colours, first thing when I get back home; my home, that stays orange and pink and gold. My home retains its posture, come summer or fall. It keeps its colours, just as orange, red and yellow. It tries, but it turns white sometimes, on the edges of its mould. Some things never should have changed, but they did, and now there have been white flowers in our home this winter, and the last. I guess now, some things will never change.

iii. I miss that feeling of warmth in my eyes; most nights, I just feel the wetness of dew. I miss the feeling of a cooling breeze at dusk, and in the depths of the day, I crave the presence of that familiar warmth. I still try to do more than survive. I carry within me the oceans that swept me away last winter when I look out into the face of an unfamiliar sun, in a city that grows on me more and more with each ray of light; each sweeping gust of air. I love, and I live, and I too think I have changed. But in my love, it's oceanic loss and my quests to find newer happiness, *I guess some things will always stay the same.*

Autumn

of fiery Reds, of lustrous Golds;

a Lifetime of Remembrance

Autumnal

Messy are the days that are set against
this sky with its heart of gold.

Against my cold, cold fingertips,
down to the cold of my sordid bones.

Peaceful is the world
where autumn leaves are wet
before they even touch the moss-covered floor,
under the stomp of leathered boots, upon muzzled stone;
scarves and sweaters catching the fall
of the coming winter's sighs, and a warm, breezy love,
all this while, warming every gust of cold.

It is hard to put into words
what it feels like to feel this mess of a morning
wash away with this autumnal tide;
clusters of leaves under my leathered calves
with roses on the side.

And skies,

the kind I have never seen,

heavy with such sorrow.

And still, life goes on,

and even a messy morning weathers on;

pushed beyond the seasons with gusts of gold,

rolling stones into the unknown.

Into autumnal reds,

and a sky of silver,

with a heart of gold.

Shambles

Yet, my feelings feel so old

Yet, an ancient, trickling rush of gold

Against this bottomless cold,

a burning in my lungs as I breathe in

the breeze of this frigid sky.

Senselessly beguiling, I already know,

I will miss these cobbles

when this time has passed and gone;

So, I milk the scent out of the rain

with every drop that falls,

and I see right through my angelity,

This time, I will try to be a god

as I will keep flowers, pink and blue,

out of a bottle of wine by my window booth,

maybe a newer, fresher splash of paint

by my bedside too.

The same as always,

but happier too.

Breathing in the freshness of this dappled,

English pebble sky.

Traces

Traces of your fingers on the entirety of my life.

The thread work of your fatherhood all over the span of my life, the decades that have come to be and are yet to come. To exist, as lovingly, in the same home where we shared the last twenty-one and a half years of our lives, our chapter, together. To lift myself even as I crumble at this familiar daydream I carry with me wherever I go, waking up so peacefully from a short sleep on the living room couch to you pinching the curves of my cheek. Traces of that memory, the white purity of fatherhood on the soft fragments of a peaceful sleep;

to have *only that* as a memory.

Even now, 7 months later, I find it hard to look inside your room without remembering you asleep. I get drunk, and all I think of is my father feeling momentarily at peace. Traces of your loitering love, your footsteps when I am alone.

Traces, are all I have left of you

Traces of your love, lacing the rest of my life.

White Light

Dreamcatcher in the front view line,

the scent of floral soliloquies,

and the bite-sized beads of summer fruit in your golden,

sweet glass of wine.

It is the crown of sunshine

that breaks through every time;

every time we are not forced to smile,

the line of white

that bounces off that golden mind.

The white light of stars that have come to align,

bound by a thin,

metal,

invisible string of gold.

When the Purple Heather Blooms

When the cold of September trespasses its way into the lightening cool of a summer day, when the trains feel as empty as the long, winding road, that eventually comes roaming this way, that is where I see, *lost*, loneliness pave the way on these rocks.

And the sky feels cold, even in the throes of July.

Autumn sheds a whisper, but a whisper so ancient is even louder than a cry; the flickering ends of summer, leaving in heather by the tracks outside.

Purples that darken, as the dark months make their way home.

Train Tracks

No, it did not seem to swallow me whole,

when the plane touched down on some grassy shore.

It feels like autumn, in the whisper

of when a train leaves its stop, and the silence falls like young spring snow.

I am sailor of the choices I make, and every track here leads off the map, off this road.

I belong to the carriages of life that take me onboard,

And I listen to the bluebells on that empty train track.

And in the silence of what gives,

and what always takes away,

I hear the song of the wind set sail

on this trail of daffodil and stone.

In its absence, I listen for some old-town,

rustic score;

I listen for the jingling, jangling

hooting hum

of an old soul's weary bones.

Tea Light

You were always adamant in your belief, in the testimonies of your religiosity, and in your hope that I would adhere to the same.

But,

I do not believe in an interventionist God.

I do, however, believe in faith. The golden light of it washing over you. Maybe you felt the same, but I do not think you understood that maybe I did too.

We are Hindu by birth, by our choice to adopt this sect of faith we were born into. But faith is universal. You may not have said it often, but you believed in the power of prayer, maybe above even the power of fate. Prayer, that exists in more paths than just the one you choose. So, today, I stood in front of an altar, in a Protestant church, and I read a sign over and over that said something like this- "Light a candle for someone you miss. It's Free." Below, a rack of tea lights, waiting to join the twelve that were already lit. I stared at that sign for a few minutes, rolling the thought of being the only one in that room to not contemplate the magnificence of the ceiling's architecture, but instead, to stare deeply, thoroughly, into the pull towards a prayer.

A moment of remembrance.

I think of you every day, at the precipice of every missed opportunity to tell you about my life, the way I get to tell Mom. I honour you, in my own way, but I have not honoured you in the ways of a tradition since the bitterness of last January. So, today, I lit a flame, a tiny tea light, in the middle of that massive, magnificent Cathedral. For you. And I wept as I walked back out into the rain.

For this lifetime of remembrance.

How many candles do I light?

I can feel you missing me

As much as I miss you.

Known

There was a time

when life was so broken-hearted, the days watched with *eyes painted blue*. And all in all, there was nothing that would stop the clocks from turning time, time and again, away from you. But here I sit, and the evening sky whispers, glances through eyes painted in shades of violet under gold; I cannot move away, it seems, so I choose to move on with you.

Because such is this universe,

such is life.

I listen to my own fable, and every day I realise, that there is no escaping what is unknown. There is no answer, and there is no real sense of the absolute score. *But*

There is this vision,

and there is this light, there is the morning sun and the twilight before night;

there is grief in *knowing,* alright,

but then there is salvation in learning to love the world outside closed doors, and there is purpose

in saving the ones you can afford.

Without loss, there is no remembrance of love.

Summer

Of Sunlight, of Molten Gold;

tracing back the threads of our Existence.

Summer Peak

Slowly,

slowly,

all the light that once was

is starting to make its way home.

Slowly, the birds and the hornets

shake the wind right off their bare bones and

finally,

in all totality

spring sheds its lukewarm notes onto summer's

evergreen and gold.

All the light that once was

is melting over emerald trees and water worn stone,

Up on the grey goose's back, *it found its way back home.*

Fragrance

You could be my evergreen, my field of wildflowers
in the Indian summer fold;
I could be the exact shade of peony,
that compliments your midnight, Parisian glow.
You could be my sea breeze,
my salted spell spraying from the ocean floor;
I am willing to let you take me back to my shores,
the ones I have strayed from for so long,
and I could take you to and back from the moon.

You give me a deck of irises,
ones I have written into my grief before,
and I give you sunshine,
a head full of red and copper that brings to mind
a special shade of warmth.
I could be your favourite fragrance,
your seashell shade of sparkling blue,

and you could be my olive green,

a shade of serenity,

I never quite felt I knew;

and together, we could ride the breeze with bits of lavender,

roses and thyme,

the kind that set the scene, of a loving

hearth and home.

Artistry

I have felt more in moments of fragility,
in their ripples, soft and crystal,
that fill the spaces in pools of cool, godly tranquillity,
than I have in the sonic voltage of this fiery,
mechanical world.
Joy within the shading, joy within the hum,
the music of our lives has been written for ages
and over and over has been sung;
and we still find ways to love it anyway.
I am drawn to Monet in his perfumed artistry,
I am drawn to Antonoff in his ability
to put into song all the colours under the moon,
and I find myself moved by the fuchsia pink
of the folklore dress I saw swirling,
bright like the pink under a midnight sun.

I am drawn to artists
fabling their artistry.
whether black or gushing colour,
laced, with woven gold.

Heart on My Sleeve

Wild, wild children, are never as fragile
as the beauty they tend to forgo.
Wild, wild leaves,
freedom in the autumn breeze,
the last fringe of gold before the cold,
December snow.
Wild music
Winding trees
Wild heart
You belong among the wildflowers
on the fringes of the big city, *stark*,
you belong among the suitors
that come with their open sleeves adorning their hearts;
you wear yours with a band of starlight,
with silver that outshines the midnight sun.

And I want to be the one
with youth written boldly over my chest,
with my heart tattooed

next to the roses that in remembrance, I wear.

I want to be the one you think of when you say

“You could always follow the beat

of her unveiled heart”.

Ghosts

It feels so distant, all of a sudden,
this feeling of *knowing* what now is no more.
It feels so familiar, now more than before,
the *easiness* of never letting go;
and suddenly, now
there is no remorse.

Now,
I have learnt to live with ghosts.

And promises run weathered,
ivy grows over watered stone;
those dragons and mothers and soothsayers,
all tell the same tale, yet tell nothing at all.
Now the story goes on, as ever before.

Now,
It has learnt to stay its course.
Now, I learn to break bread with your ghosts.

Northern Light

Alone and lonesome, seated on the edge of a settling light. Alone and shrouded, under the vastness of the heavenly sky, there is a cosmos; a cluster of a billion setting suns. They have been there before, they will be there after the last of us die, and even then, we cannot begin to comprehend this angelic choir of a billion shining sentinels.

How they blink together and send *this* message, meant to stay there over the passage of infinite, lonesome time.

How rare and beautiful it is to even begin to exist

When so much has existed before the semblance of our lives. I never thought the universe was made just to be seen by my eyes. I have always tried to find the words for this, but right now, I really think the universe is bigger, even bigger than this moment in time; than this moment that stands before an age of history and passed, weathered, wrinkled time. Still golden in the midst of its hourglass end. Small and insignificant, watching the majesty of this worldly sky that stays as it is, as it ever will stay over the rest of our lives. Infinity times infinity.

Infinity times infinity, the loneliest words to ever come out of this world.

Creation

At the very beginning,

do you see?

A lone acacia,

two more across a lone, bare

primordial land,

and the thrust of brown, green and gold

splattered across acre,

upon acre,

upon *infinite*.

All that the light touches is where

it all began,

all where the light reaches,

reaches out its incandescent hand,

is all that ever was,

and all that will ever be.

Is all that the world will ever have,

still,

silent,

lonesome acacias

at the barrel of all creation.

Summer is a Symphony Of

Summer is a vacuum of cherry pies and cherry skies and moonlight that stays vacant till the sun rolls over the edge of the cerulean seas, till it beckons the taste of a monstrous heat, the kind that pools the nerves into a single cube in our glasses of lemonade ice. Summer is a long, long solstice of love and heartstrings and the crust of a sobering shadow along the edges of the incoming night, the incoming autumnal cold. But, until then, summer is many things.

At its most plastic, it is red solo cups and barbecues, it is cherry lips and cherry cones and shorts and bodies that run hotter than the cerulean, sobering gold. Summer is cool mornings, for some of us, and the cool, sparkling twangs of the rolling stones. Summer is a symphony of love, like I said, but also a spree of high school love and old country songs.

Summer is a solstice of fleeting, footloose song and dance.

It is pure,

and evergreen,

saturated joy.

Monsoon: ii

i. The last time I wrote of monsoon,
I wrote a verse on its subtlety,
the sublime colour of the sky and its pattering drops;
I wrote of love in the form of a dewy fog,
that wraps itself around July's earthen rain.

Through the harshness of the flooding rain,
I wrote of softness, the kind that condenses into the skies.

ii. Over the course of a year, its months,
and their bouts of graceful, slashing rain,
I think I saw that same fog rise up
to neon and angelic, poppy-coloured skies;
I think I felt the same fingertip traces of love
that I fell for years ago, and maybe that is why
I fall in love with the monsoon, every time I come home to July.

Somehow, within the colours of the draining sky,
I find new love in them, all over again.

Worshipper

Stumbled on a piece of fresh sunlight,

and hopelessly degenerate, you stumbled a step more, before your fall;

You missed your grace and ages ago, your call,

and never will a bud of rosary bloom

just for you.

Has the light ever shone on you,

in your moment of Everest decline?

Has a healer of faith ever looked at you,

and in all benediction, reclined?

I pray to you, and in your misty hair, I resign.

You are my monsoon

the freshest breath of air

I have ever had the pleasure of calling mine.

I dance in the pallor of your summer rain

your bangles ripple, and I hear your name

in a songbird's throw of mercurial delight.

Don't pray to me, live for the love you receive in kind.

Don't pray for me, just keep me dancing

on the edges of your mind.

What I Think About While Romanticising the Tube

The London underground is a festering, swarming horde of what we all know city life to be- bustling, pushy, ever so many crowds of people with all sorts of stories, and of all sorts of humanity. On a crowded part of the day, which is most of the weekend and office commute times, it takes strength to be able to maintain composure while being pushed together and stuffed into a metal compartment, while struggling to maintain balance and your belongings and not to mention, stress levels, especially when you are running late to be wherever the day has called for.

It can be awful. It is hard to breathe and hard to not feel absolutely icky as you sweat your breakfast out amongst ALL these people, of whom some are just as crabby and far less composed than you. It is hard, until that one stop where most of this crowd has been waiting to get off, and at long last, one final round of shoving each other around brings with it a quite literal, breath of air. It is cooling and suddenly space seems to be almost infinite, and it really does feel like this big metaphor for life when a time of turbulence eases into a period where you can stretch your limbs and your cramped up soul, and notice the rest of the world and how it fares.

You look up, look around, and since the crowd has gone, you see pieces of what it means to be human right here, in this compartment of a random underground train.

You notice families with children whose decibel levels were ungodly moments ago, but who are now snuggling up to their fathers, these grown men looking relaxed as their child holds their hand out of peace, not discomfort. A young woman to the right, so hassled five minutes ago, but now looking at her phone and beaming, unknowingly playing with her engagement ring as she does. Force of habit, *force of love*. Always too, there are the ones that bring out a book, or a little journal where they write down their daily affirmations with little hearts and stars at the seams of the pages. Speaking of hearts, dressy duos of friends are littered around, chatting about the Aperols they are looking forward to when they reach Soho, while two lovers sitting parallel to them enjoy a moment of silence. She, clearly uncomfortable with the crowds when she got on, now smiles slightly as her boyfriend holds her hand and strokes this head of gold on his shoulder; a head that moments ago ran with lines of stress but now enjoys this sweet little bit of human touch, almost comparable to the children further away from them who now rest on their parents' arms. People, when we aren't walking over each others' feet to try and fit ourselves into an undersized world, always show the sweetness we are so naturally capable of when we find a second to breathe. And there's something important in that sentiment, especially if one is at a loss to understand why we all work together; how we mirror love, and comfort, off of each other.

I was standing behind a woman with a huge "ॐ" hanging in gold off her ears, crushed between her and three other people and a very uncomfortable slate of metal behind my back. Once I managed to breathe, and take in all the micro-behaviours in this little ecosystem we all found ourselves in, I peered into what she was so intently typing out on her phone. A flaw of what comes out of the human need to know each other- I am guilty of a spot of nosiness. I watched as she typed in lines and lines of gratitude, and I thought it was precious that the first second she got to herself on this crowded train, she decided to write down what she was grateful for that day. "*A home*", she wrote. "*The best home I could ever ask for*". Just like her, I thought, I'd write about what made me happy today. And I wrote about how people, when left alone, give you a little sneak into their own little worlds, and how it is always a world strung together with the absence of malice.

And then we all part ways, and the whole thing begins all over again.

Sidenote: must also observe the flow of hands and smiles on the New York subway. I'm sure it mimics the little bits of beauty on the tube.

The Anglerfish

The Internet, as it stands today, is a cesspool of hatred; a melting pot of the Right, the Left and everyone else in there, wedged in between. I hate it sometimes, like when someone speaks of the love of their lives and twenty others say that they belong in hell, for having two pairs of breasts, in the centre of their love, for spreading hate against those who deny their right to live and to be loved, and sometimes, they try and convince me that I am in the wrong. But I have always said this is just one half, and the other half came to my side of the internet

in the shape of an Anglerfish;
the one that floated
towards the sun.

She didn't mean to, but there she was, 6500 miles from her darkened house, and suddenly ALL these people gathered, saying they cried over her journey towards the Light.

The Light

Because we are all Icarus, we are all Orpheus, and we are all people, who, despite Hate and Bigotry and Vice, look at a darkened, misshapen fish, floating up the depths of her own demise, and say "*That's Life*". That's poetry, and that's romance within the unknown; that's us agreeing despite our own darkened, misshapen souls that We ALL, despite our allegiance to foreigner suns and foreigner gods,

yearn to touch The Light

in our final moments of demise.

Molten

In the melting colours of the sun,

I find that I beget the sounds of this setting world,

onto the endless bridge between space and time.

Etched against the orange, pink,

ethereal palette of settling sky,

I pray to never be left without your canvas

by my side;

In this synapse of molten love,

I only pray

Don't fall away from me.

Couldn’t You?

I don’t know what to do with all the space

I still have left from your passing through.

I feel the windows shake and shudder, raging

from all the tidal love they are meant to hold.

I was almost 22

And now dreams are the only real memories

I have left of you.

couldn’t you have stayed

a little bit longer?

Shallows / गहराइयां

In the shallows of this well-trodden shore,
fragmented seashells mirroring the shattered bones
of that one grey morning, six months ago;
I feel my cesspool blues
churn out foams of turquoise;

after the dark of the setting sea, it's nice to finally feel
a salt breeze brush against the depths of an age's demise.

और इन्हीं गहराइयों में दिखे वो खोए हुए रास्ते
और वो ही खोयी-खोयी शाम,
इतना समय होने पर भी
ये गहराइयां खामोश रहती है कहा।

किसी दिन वापस आने पर, इसी नज़ारे में मिलेगा
वो ही डूबता सूरज,
उसका लहरों पे निशान।

Next time,

I hope to trace these depths,

with the shallows of a mended heart.

Spring

Of Equinox, of Pink light;

setting forth across the Endless Cosmic Sea

Spring Equinox

I doodle flowers in my sidelines, and the world dots herself with crocuses,

pinks and yellows,

pale and gentle dawns.

Sweet and feeble, like a doe rising with her crown of thorns,

spring rises in her equinox,

and I press petals in my notebooks again.

A Dream That Was Not My Own

It is the walking, treading, line you toe
between this Earth and the shallows of your ghosts,
stepping stone upon stepping stone of hollow, clouded glass.
It is lucidity, is it not?
To layer a *Dream* upon sorrow,
and wake up with a feeling sinking further down than ever before because,
in my sleep,
I thought, "God";
Maybe I was happier when I could feel myself fall
without caring about hitting any sort of solid ground.
Maybe I felt free because

falling along the tract of the Milky Way,
through the Universe's cord and its infinite Vertebrae

I was uplifted, not happy nor alone;
just treading the milky stepping stones
above the shallows of the ocean world I find myself awake in,
floating, and submerged.

Sunblind: ii

For the warm, lingering gold of Christmas lights,

for the freezing kiss of winter that kept alive the crevices of the mind;

grateful, the trees may rejoice,

for laying to rest this past,

and coming back to life.

And in the last sugared whispers

of February's dotted skies,

comes the song of Spring with her may-flower hair

and skin of dappled sunlight;

in this miracle that flows, I feel sunblind;

sunrises paling in the constant grace of your touch.

Wake Up, It's 2020!

Wake up! And it is one of those days, that you just *know* would have been perfect,

if you had eaten enough at the start. But now, mistake's been made, and off I go- it is Spring outside. It is spring in the temperature, in the wind and in how it doesn't freeze you to your core- it feels perfectly cool, in this sweater I have on. I have loved days like these ever since I can remember, because days like these come rushing through the door with this burst of sound and energy- with neon blue ribbons of rock'n'roll synergy curling their way around me and around my scarf, as it blows in the breeze. It *feels* more than spring now, almost like Summer is just on its way. I loved summer as a child because during court-mandated holidays, it felt like every day was Sunday,

and my parents were home.

Today felt like I was *lucky.* I was lucky because I got to wake up late and get to class on my own time. Lucky because even though my head felt worn down, I got to walk back home and click pictures of cherry blossoms in front of a melting pot of sun. Lucky, because, I got to come home, light a candle, switch on my fairy lights and watch my pink sheets turn gold under the sunlight- just like in my living room back home, where the evening sun hits the sofas and the walls before it finally dips on down beyond the sky. Luckier, even, because I got to put my laptop on charge and crawl into those pink sheets for a late-day house-cat nap. And in my sleep, I felt like I was made of summer too.

I felt like summer too because a single bird outside let out soft calls, and I could hear the water running in the river next to my home. Because I could picture a creek, not far from where I was, or maybe it was somewhere in Ireland, where at this point in time the water would be softly gurgling in the woods, and the sunlight falling would be dappled, soft, and benign. Because simultaneously, days and naps like this always take me back to 2020, when lockdown left us all satiated for a moment, and I could just fall deeply asleep on my own dappled, sunlit, living room couch. Sorrow, dappled now. *Because naps like these always end with the phantom of my father's soft pinch on my cheek as I wake.*

I wish I woke up back in 2020, when I did not have this thought that other kids get to save their dads, and I don't. But I wake up, and it's 2025, and I am lucky because my room is glowing from those fairy lights, and my pink sheets are golden and see-through. I am in England, and it is the dawn of Summer, and this is where poets get to write about the world in all its softness, golden summer love. Tomorrow, I will eat enough and take out time to read a book,

before the hollows,

the phantoms,

and the softness of this world

make me too tender for words again.

Known: ii

A quiet evening, beckoning sunlit sight, even as it pales, it dawns,

blossoms like a blue, clouded rose,

lilac, cool, against the periwinkled sky.

It feels good to be home,

back to a sky that even today

sets in colours that are known,

that are not found anywhere beyond this small,

bit of coast.

I am back where I started, 5 years ago,

and what a love it is

to be back where the sky is known.

Sailor's Moon

Maybe it is a simple twist of fate, or maybe

I wove the knots to this simple gold chain,

all on my own.

Maybe,

it was never up to me at all, but up to what tests

the betterment of my solitude.

What if I swam away from my shores, only to come floating back to you?

What if I am a sailor, guided only by the precarious moon;

guided to be free, only under your beck

and calling tide.

Infinity

There is something truly belittling, only in the kindest, *most wondrous way*, about having the luxury of looking through the looking glass; an endless gaze that brings with it an endless infinity out there, waiting in the vast, VAST, stretch of cold, powder-blue sky. And there is only so much to make sense of- the breeze, the cold, the sky; the soaring incandescent soul of the sun that has shone just like this forever, and ever before.

My true North have always been the chemtrails, all alone,

across the lonely cold of the sky.

And this is infinity, and it is a sight so rare, but it exists, and I see it sometimes like I'd see an old school friend; it leaves me belittled as ever before. It makes me wonder if there will ever come a time when I look at a chemtrail trying to cover the miles before it all and not have to think about how small,

and lonely,

it must feel; how lost,

as I watch it leave its linear, sunset glow. Watch it cover the endless, its own unknown, slowly covering the millimetres against the inky, black sea night.

And for that stretch of parallel collision,

for that shared, beautiful colliding time,

I swear I can feel the sky, the sun, the blue, the cold.

And I feel infinite too.

Spectacle

Watching myself, who knows if *sober* is really the way to come close to the magnitude of this world, to the magnitude of our times? I am not unhinged, nor am I come loose- is there something so wrong with not being able to see God if not under the influence of *music* so heady, so dark and full of waves like wine?

Watching myself, maybe I am close to the setting of Empires, the setting of Moon Gods; the glorious chorus of angels with the gold of their heavenly crowns falling, *dripping*, over their lost daughters and prodigal sons. Maybe I do understand their Christian God, who may be a little less opaque than my own.

Maybe I see why there is always a remembrance of hope

How can there be nothing, when such beauty still exists in this world?

Past Few Months

I have spent the past few months
trying to assess the fragmented stature of my core,
living my days in ways I have always lived by before,
noticing the fragments of my citric world
I thought previously to be ripe, fulfilling and whole.

I spent days sitting still while the world moved by,
back and forth,
while I tried to fill my cracks with lines of solid gold
and failed even to wake up to my favourite songs.
I spent the past few months trying to reclaim myself
on the shore of a broken coastline.

But it has been months, and I am here now.
I am here now,
and it has been days since my last fleet of desolating storms.
it has been days of sunshine and waves and colours seeping
into my periphery, a kaleidoscope making its way
back through the shitstorm,

and I can finally feel the cracks glisten white with gold.

I can run to songs down my broken shore, and in these past few months,

I have only known salvation to its core.

I am here now, here with it all,

and these past few months

have been set free.

Sea Prayer

Some days I see an image, clear,
of the moment after I die.
I will find my place of rest,
Myself,
along the shore of an endless coastline;
sea foam lapping at the tips of my feet.

I imagine you will be there too,
waiting,
and finally, we will sit,
by the oceans you and I have always loved,
and I will tell you about all the things I wish
you were there with me to see.

Acknowledgements

I would like to start by thanking my family for uplifting one another with love, and for giving me the opportunity to explore the world outside of home. Thank you for giving me an endless resource of kindness and resilience.

To my friends in Delhi, thank you for giving me this vibrance to come back home to. The love I write of would not exist without you. To my friends across the world- Dublin, London and York would be meaningless without you. The experiences that inspire me would be meaningless without you.

Lastly, I extend my thanks to BlueRose Publications for giving me this platform to put my work out into the world. Truly, it takes a village.